Patterns
of the Heart

Gentle Thoughts on Aging

Becci Bookner

ISBN 0-978-0-9819951-1-3

Second Edition, June 2009

Printed in the United States of America
on acid-free paper

Prepress by Author's Corner, LLC

Cover layout and interior layout by Joyce Dierschke

Published by:

Author's Corner, LLC
7978 Coley Davis Road, Suite 101
Nashville, Tennessee 37221

With Heartfelt Gratitude

This book is dedicated to Paul, my husband, whose love for life and deep appreciation for literature inspired me to write; and...

To my sister, Bettye, whose support and encouragement to achieve my dreams were and are unconditional and unwavering.

Thank you both for a million things that were patterns of love on display and continue to be an inspiration to me and many others.

Becci

Table of Contents

Gifts from Grace

On September 24, 1913, a little girl was born. Her parents named her Grace ... a blessing in itself to be given that name. But the bigger blessing is how that little girl created such a life for herself that she is indeed as the song goes ... Amazing Grace. Now, almost a century later, the Grace of this story continues to live life and each day she teaches lessons about living to those lucky enough to be a part of her world.

During these ninety-two years, Grace was no stranger to difficulty and disappointment. Her husband died unexpectedly at age fifty-one, leaving her with five children and a background which did not include work experience outside the home. Twice cancer made an untimely visit. She had every opportunity to become unhappy, bitter, and unfulfilled. But not Grace!

Was it the name her parents chose that charted the life course of her special ability to remain happy and genuine? Webster defines "grace" as ... seemingly effortless beauty, charming or pleasing quality, divine love and protection given to mankind by God, and a short prayer said at mealtime. Wow! Grace is all of those things and more. Even "the short prayer at mealtime" is one of the dearest gifts she shares with those at her table.

By her example, Grace has lots to say about what we women have been doing and promoting since the advent of the "liberated woman" in the sixties and seventies. Those of us who think we are so unique, so modern, so educated, so professional, so much stronger in mind and body than the women of our parents' generation may be surprised to discover some of the "gifts from Grace."

Being independent at age ninety-two is strength in the purest sense. With arthritis and a host of other health challenges, Grace still measures her success by a morning routine of makeup, earrings, and in choosing an outfit that reflects her graciousness and joy at being blessed by God with another day of life on this earth. Even today her home is decorated for each season and the dining room table is always set for company. At ninety-two, she can put outfits together and buy items on sale that really work for her.

My life has been blessed to know Grace for many years. Yet, it is only during the last ten years that I have come to really know her. We once were just mother and daughter, but now we are best friends in the most wonderful way. We have spent more time going to the grocery store, out to breakfast, out to get our nails done, taking day trips, and spending quiet time working in her flower gardens than we did in all the first fifty years of my life.

In each of the most precious and memorable times of the last few years, I come away with a deeper appreciation for just how tough this woman is and has been all her life. She has a fierce determination to remain engaged in life even as her world gets a bit smaller. She may not drive her car, but with a driver, that car allows her to stay connected to her family, her community, and her church. Just being parked in the driveway is her statement that she is still in charge!

She loves to cook, shop, and talk on the phone. At night because she lives alone, she can sing hymns out of her church song book, read her Bible, and go to bed whenever she is good and ready. Just give her a baseball game on television, a fire in the fireplace and call her happy!

There has been much made of and written about the "greatest generation." They reference the proud military heroes who paid for our freedom with their lives. It is truly deserved and we honor them. Grace is also a part of that "greatest generation." The spirit of hope and the strength of character were not just endowed on the military. It is a gift from God that was poured out on men and women of our country during a special time in our history.

May God bless many daughters with

the privilege of sharing real time with a mom from that special generation whose life is a gift that gives meaning to the word compassion, mercy, courtesy and kindness, good taste and elegance.

Building a business to provide personal care for older family members was a gift unwrapped while caring for my aunts as they aged. But it is the time with Grace, my mother, that is the real gift... the gift of sharing a special time in living, an opportunity to experience the beauty and <u>grace</u>-ousness of aging, the <u>grace</u>-fullness of walking with slower steps, the joy of living each moment of your life with child-like enthusiasm and imagination for whatever may be just around the corner.

Thanks, Mom! I love you!

Heirloom family photo of Grace (left front) standing in front of her parents. Even as a young child, she was blessed with a special family and parents that loved her dearly.

A special day for Grace at her graduation from eighth grade. Beautifully dressed for the occasion and radiant with her special ability to be genuine and poised.

This treasured photo of Grace at age 21 is a tribute to
her seemingly effortless beauty, charm, and the pleasing
quality of her nature.

Grace, now wife and mother of two children, pictured here sharing a special Mother's Day with her mother-in-law, also a woman of strength and resilience.

Memorable times with her family created the fabric of her life. In this photo, Grace is surrounded by her father, three sisters, and two daughters. The author is sitting on her knee.

Grace, charming and beautiful at age sixty, sharing a special day at her daughter's wedding.

One of Grace's favorite photographs. After nearly a century, she continues to give meaning to the words compassion, good taste, and elegance.

Attitude
of
Altitude

In case you missed last Sunday's paper, there were some exciting numbers about people in the second fifty years of birthdays! If you combine the age groups of people over fifty, there are about 26,180 of us right here. Strength, based on numbers, confirms a *senior* power base emerging in its role and definition in community life.

While the numbers are a powerful message, there is also a growing sense of *"attitude"* and *"altitude"* that just might change the image of this group over the next few years. As you sip on a cup of hot tea or coffee and enjoy a gorgeous October afternoon in middle Tennessee, without realizing it, you may be demonstrating an *attitude* that is a must for feeling good about yourself, about life, and about your age.

Consider for a moment the word *attitude*. This word has recently become something used to describe a negative, troublesome approach to thinking and behaving that gets in one's way of acceptable performance. However, on this special afternoon and within this amazing group of over twenty six thousand of us, someone with *"an attitude"* is an unexpected treasure that deserves to be polished, praised, and used as a benchmark for successful living.

This *attitude* is the self reliant, independent thinking, "I will do it myself" spirit that burned in the hearts of those who carved out our country. Quite different, wouldn't you say, from the *attitude* of "let the government, let the doctor, and let anyone but me be responsible for what is happening!" Some folks never bought this negative unproductive approach to life for one minute. Thank goodness for that!

Now think about the word *altitude*. It conjures up thoughts of mountain climbers and test pilots or bald eagles soaring in the clouds. A personal altitude gauge is as important as a positive attitude, particularly if you are the oldest person on your street or in your apartment complex. It is just as important if you are just one of the twenty-six thousand men and women over fifty in our area.

Each of us has a certain responsibility to demonstrate this "*attitude of altitude*" that gift wraps life with joy, is contagious with enthusiasm, and refuses to accept aging as a punishment. You are the window of opportunity for others to see for themselves that the gift of living does not stop with grey hair or hearing aids. One of the local golfers can tell you about an *attitude of altitude.* He is seventy-three years old and rides his motorcycle to the golf course every weekend.

If the sum of what people expect about *aging* is based on television spots and hearsay, it is easy to accept that life, after your AARP card, is a series of pain pills and broken hips, of depression and hopelessness! Some may even think that if you do not eat at McDonald's or play sports, you must live on social security allotments and buy Depends.

What a bunch of bunk! So what if you do! What does it matter if you don't hear as good or walk as fast or have fingers bent with arthritis?

The real message to send is that this

group of over 26,000 men and women in our town have traveled more than any group, are the best educated, have more opportunities, are in the best health, have had more experience in business, have voted in more elections, have experienced more historical events, and have more money in the bank and cash available than any other generation in the history of the United States. They know how to stretch a dollar further than any other group of consumers. Many may even still have the first dollar ever earned and this is not all bad.

The challenge to ourselves and all we meet along the way is to bring down the curtain on the too often accepted description of aging as in the book *Enjoy Old Age*. "... Old persons have been crotchety, stingy, boastful, boring, demanding, and arrogant. You may be surprised at how easy it is to play the part that way. The audience expects such a performance." Not any more!

Frances Weaver is one of my favorite authors and our "attitude of altitude" winner of the week. She puts it like this... "Being older nowadays is not for sissies. It is for those self-starters who can learn to fly kites, go back to school, and re-evaluate who they are and where they want to go after the death of a spouse – or the emptying of a noisy, child-dominated household." Way to go, Frances!

Until next time, God bless.

Merging

Sometimes, there are stories we hear that just seem to linger on in our thoughts. That's the case of one I heard recently. A family had noticed that one of their favorite aunts had stopped attending the family functions and get-togethers. Since all were quite fond of the aunt, they decided that someone should pay a visit to her and make sure she would plan to be with them for the next get together ... so one of them did.

After the perfunctory small talk, the conversation centered on why she had not chosen to be with the family as she had always been in the past. She did not give them much of a response. So the questions continued. Finally, the aunt said, "I can't merge." "You can't do what?" the questioning relative exclaimed. "I can not merge anymore!" What a profound announcement!

The aunt was, of course, referring to the fact that she had to drive the car to be with the family. She would be forced to "merge" into and out of the traffic patterns on the various highways to arrive across town. She could not do that anymore. Indeed, this unexpected answer for that family is *a green light* for us to consider situations we may ourselves face from day to day.

The act of "merging" is a necessary skill in all stages of life. Example, youngsters learn appropriate behavior when company comes. They "merge" into the adult world with certain expected behaviors and for a defined period of time. Then, they slip back into the comfort zone of childhood and run off to play outside or in their room.

Families have rituals and customs peculiar to them, and them alone. These are significant for the newly weds who must "merge" traditions and ideas if the marriage and relationship is to grow and develop into a successful emotional union of two people.

Some of us are attempting to "merge" into the computer age. Wow! To make this "merger" even more of a personal challenge, the computer whizzes who are teaching us are twenty to thirty or more years younger than are we. This can be a particularly difficult merger of different worlds, languages, and skills.

Corporate mergers, stock mergers, household mergers and the like are in the news and up for discussion at business lunches, dinners, board rooms and breakfast bars. There are notions of "can not merge," "shouldn't merge," "won't merge," and, of course, "don't merge" or "I wish I had merged."

The aunt in the story who couldn't merge in traffic can teach us several lessons about ourselves as we add candles to our birthday cake. Not being able to "merge" is a fact of life at every age, not just among the people who may not be comfortable driving in fast-paced style traffic. At each stage of life, there are accessories and gadgets available to help "youngsters" learning to ride a bicycle to "oldsters" using a walker with wheels.

Just because you can't merge does not mean you can't take a taxi! Recognizing a "merging" limitation or restriction should be followed by finding an alternate route.

At these two wonderfully unique times

in our lives and all the times in between, life gives us certain boxes of tools. These "toolboxes for merging" allow us to make necessary mid-course adjustments for what we do and how we choose to continue taking advantage of each day we are given on this earth. While there are many items worthy of celebration in this toolbox for "merging," the one that gets the spotlight today is the "cane."

"Canes" can go by many names and can come in a multitude of styles, degrees of artwork and practicality. Walking canes are the ultimate merging device. The utility and remarkable recorded history of walking canes dates back to the earliest biblical times. Canes are the eyes for the blind and essential support for the weak. A cane can be an extension of an arm to deliver a tap on the back or a poke in the ribs. When inverted, they are a most effective "grabber" and hook. Walking canes may actually be more accommodating than training wheels on a bicycle or bumpers on a car.

What could be sweeter than a designer walking cane for ladies complete with color coordinated ruffles and bows? Is there a beaded and sequined walking cane waiting to be created for the next gala evening in town? If there is, it will be the talk of the event and will be quite a show stopper!

Lucky will be the grandmother whose family bestows on her this elegant gift for "merging." Even luckier still will be, the family whose grandmother receives this cane with great satisfaction and then uses it!

The rules of the road are simple: Life is

great at all of the stages we are privileged to experience it.

God bless and "keep on merging."

Memory to Memories

You may recall that rule in English grammar about making a singular word plural by changing the "y" to an "I" and then adding "es!" You can change the word "memory" to "memories" by using this rule. But this transformation creates two words whose meanings can be worlds apart.

There is something very interesting about how *memories* can bring a smile to a face or a bit of a warm feeling to a heart. They can instantly bring back that special fragrance of grandpa's aftershave or the particular taste of that favorite dish your mom prepared. How can these sensations and feelings be stored so carefully and completely in our memory bank as though it were only yesterday?

Someone said that... "One of the most moving aspects of life is how long the deepest memories stay with us." Memories are truly one of the most wonderful parts of life. There is little wonder that we concern ourselves so much with this amazing function of the human brain!

The word "memory" has been the subject of a variety of critical analyses recently. It has become a buzz word as we have learned more about how this essential mental function relates to the process in life we call *aging*.

There are plenty of myths about life during "the second half" that deserves to be questioned. The reality about memory may just be one of the most important issues to address as we plan for a healthy and happy journey toward the big *one hundred*.

In the grind of day to day living, for
some reason, it has become so easy to
talk about how much we or those we love
are "forgetting these days." This is not to
minimize the reality of serious memory
problems which are associated with
illnesses. However, a change of attitude
toward older family members should
definitely be one that is more similar to
the way we teach and encourage our
youngsters, perhaps!

We can begin by thinking about how
truly amazing our sense of memory really
is. It is faster, more sophisticated, more
flexible, and more "user-friendly" than the
finest computer yet made, or ever to be
made in the foreseeable future. The amount
of information that can be stored in our
memory is *unlimited*. Researchers of memory
have said that by age seventy we have

literally millions of memories stored in our memory bank.

Just like the computer, the more memory stored, the more time it takes to retrieve information. Apply this concept to a person. By age seventy, for example, you may have met and have known hundreds of more people than you ever knew at age thirty-five. Immediate recall of a person's name or an event becomes a much more complicated job simply due to sheer numbers.

We rarely discard our computers just because it needs more memory! Almost with great pride, we purchase and have more memory installed. Of course, we can not purchase more memory for ourselves or our parents, but there are some things we can do.

A very important first step to sustaining and even improving memory power is to stop becoming so discouraged when we can't recall a name or a number, where we put the check book or which day it is. It may be healthier to think in terms of *memory overloaded* rather than *memory loss*!

Can you imagine the volumes and volumes of books it would take to write down all the millions of facts and feelings stored in your memory? The very concept is staggering! Wow! The longer we live, the more information we have to process.
It may just take us a little longer. If we were dealing with money instead of memory, and it took us longer to count it all because we had so much, I doubt we would be quite so discouraged!

Study after study indicates that feeling

good about yourself improves your memory.
Here is a prescription of other things you can
do to protect and improve memory, taken
from a number of very reliable sources. It is
good advice for maintaining a healthy and
happy life style, as well as a good memory
whether sixteen or ninety-six.

- *Eat well, but in moderation.*

- *Exercise the body and your memory regularly.*

- *Minimize medications when possible.*

- *Laugh and smile a lot; it is the best medicine for life.*

The great poet Cicero put it like this,
"*Memory is the treasury and guardian of all
things.*" We protect our homes and cars and
other valuable possessions we have with
insurance of all kinds. Maybe each of us
can think about how to better protect these

valuable gifts of memory and memories as we learn more about growing older.

In spite of all the rules of grammar and all the advice from pundits, may your memory and your memories continue to bring you a smile as life gets better every day.

Old Houses

44

There is something very rewarding, yet very challenging, about living in an old house. You really have to love these treasures from the past if you choose to make one the place you call home. You appreciate their peculiarities and quirks, and understand that even though they may be fabulously restored and quite beautiful, they are still and always will be an old house.

We live in one such old house built in 1897. We think it is more than lovely and still notably remarkable after one hundred years at its address in Rutherford County. It faces due south with gorgeous old maples that will turn your head every autumn. One of these historic trees, an oak, is estimated to be over 300 years old.

It has all the old house special features.
Floors that squeak, walls that are not square,
things that won't work... things you wish did
not work and, of course, noises in the night.
It has its recorded and remembered histories
of births, deaths, and all the parts of family
and community life in between. And with
all of this, we think it has an unexplainable
warmth and welcome that is all its own.

Several mornings ago, I caught a glimpse
of our old house in a setting I had not seen in
all the years we have lived here. Just before
daylight, I was walking up the back hill and
there it stood like a picture from Currier
and Ives. In that gentle, not quite light, time
of morning, the lights of the house were
pouring out through the windows, warming
the cool mist and welcoming the day! It
seemed to speak of days past and family, of
strength and history. It looked so special. It

was a scene of nostalgia and stately charm.

There are beautiful parallels between an old house that has been loved and cared for over the years and the people in our families and community who are vibrantly and joyously moving toward their 100th birthday. Some houses and some people look lonely, cold, and a little foreboding. Yet, other houses and people become more gracious and intriguing as they age. They become even more valuable and respected, more loved, and appreciated because of the continued contributions they make to others. The older they are, the more of a treasure they become.

There is no clear answer for why this happens! But our old house has taught us some pretty simple lessons about living and aging. First, we are all very much like old houses in our peculiarities and quirks, and wonder and beauty. Second, we can be proud as we age: old houses wrote the book on "wrinkles and cellulite" yet they remain beautiful. The third lesson is that on your 100th birthday you will not get that horrible bouquet of black balloons inscribed with "Over the Hill." What ever the gift, it will not have a negative theme, but will be one of great joy and support.

If your plan is to be around to celebrate the big 100th, you have to commit to withstand the test of time and weather the storms. After years of service, house paint will show signs of cellulite, wrinkling, and buckling just like alligator skin! But a fresh coat of paint can work wonders to revamp its appearance. The same thing happens to people, too. We just cover it with makeup, grow a beard or camouflage it with a huge smile that makes others forget. While having lunch recently with a friend and her mom... they shared this special thought about wrinkles. *"Wrinkles are the lines of memories past."* So it is with people and houses.

We must learn to love and appreciate the knees that squeak and backs that are less than straight. We must be determined that these peculiarities of age will not stop us from "spiffing" up every single morning and turning on that light of positive attitude and zest for life that shines through the window of our faces. We have to put our best foot forward and find the strength of will and spirit to turn on a smile those passersby will consider amazing. They just may be so inspired by this meeting that their journey in life will find a better direction and more noble course.

Just as old houses proudly reflect the past while they speak of the present and challenge the future, so must we. Antique lovers and old home preservationists will, with great passion, accomplish overwhelmingly difficult processes, and spend unlimited amounts of money to restore and revitalize these tributes from yesterday.

These remarkable efforts to rebuild and embellish houses are so similar to our own efforts to take care of ourselves. How we protect and care for this human body and maximize its ability to operate efficiently will determine how long we continue to break records of longevity. It will take time and resources to rebuild a home. It takes more time, more commitment, and more resources to maintain a healthy mind and body that will meet the challenges of the aging process.

Because of, or in spite of, our love affair with old houses, antiques, and historical sites, we know that the real treasures in our community are those who can remember Lindberg and Roosevelt, street cars and gas lights. One grandmother at age ninety wrote and had published, <u>HAYWOOD HOME: Memories of a Mountain Woman</u>. Half blind and with increasing arthritic problems, she wrote primarily for her family, hoping others would enjoy her remembrances as well.

Alice Haynes, and all others like her are not only our family and heroes, but also our treasures. In the Prologue she wrote, "... Most of what I have written is from memory. I have had a hard life, but a good life, with few regrets. This is dedicated to the people who have made my life worth living."

If children are considered our greatest natural resource, then our older family members are truly our greatest national treasure. They are here, just like the house on that special morning, proud to be a part of our life and inviting us to be a part of their special world.

God bless them all!

Borders of Golden Glow

As so many drivers know who use the interstate connecting Murfreesboro and Nashville, the drive between the two cities has become a stop-and-go process over the last few months due to construction and the increasing volume of vehicles. We can make that drive with our mind in neutral because the distance and the congestion have become somewhat routine.

Occasionally, drivers look for things to occupy them during the delays. Some use the time to think, plan or develop strategies for the next business meeting or project. Some take an uninterrupted moment to appreciate nature and think reflectively. Some listen to motivational or instructional tapes. It's been said that you could earn a college degree or master a second language if you studied during all the time spent in cars and during traffic jams. Maybe so!

Well, you might wonder what this little sermon has to do with those of us who do not drive anywhere, much less to Nashville during rush hour. Good question. There is a real connection, however. We know that traffic jams, like all situations in life, are relative and can be either a problem or an opportunity! Just this past week, during one of those "traffic jam opportunities" something really wonderful did happen!

A little background, please.

For the past few years, state government has been experimenting with gardens of wild flowers planted and maintained at several points along the section of I-24

between Nashville and Murfreesboro.
Wildflower gardens like these take several
years to mature and become beautiful. It has
been a joy to see the colors and blossoms of
the flowers and the project, itself. Even the
crews who use those huge mowers to cut and
maintain the medians and areas along side
the interstate have been on notice to take
caution when working around these gardens.

During this particular traffic delay, as I
noticed that the gardens had been cut and
cleaned for the upcoming fall season, along
the edge of the pavement and in the gravel
right beside my car was a miracle!

In the midst of the air pollution,
automobile exhaust fumes, stifling summer
heat with little or no rain, litter and the
routine grass control crews who mow,
trim, and even have been known to use

chemicals to win the war on weeds, was an unbelievably profuse border of beautiful tiny, sturdy, yellow wildflowers! We are not talking about just a few here. This yellow border of blooms went as far as my eye could see.

For lack of a scientific name, we will call them "golden glow" wildflowers. These small yellow wildflowers have not been protected, are not in a cultivated nor planned garden that receives the attention and loving respect of all who drive by. The fully blossomed little reminders of the power of nature to endure and even flourish, in adverse conditions, serve as a powerful tribute of what life and *aging* are really about. They are symbolic in their beauty and eternal in their story.

They have been cut down again and again,

yet they come back every time with even more blossoms. Now they are emerging as a "bouquet" rather than a single flower. Wow! Isn't this the story of the life of many of the friends and heroes we love and admire? Isn't this really a story about each of us?

These little miracles are a grand analogy for life and the joy of longevity. As the years pass, we survive and conquer the hard times, the pain and the hurt, the disappointment and even the loss of loved ones. We "know the road"... just like those little yellow flowers. We have been there.

Most of us, at least the fortunate ones, have tucked all those challenges away in our pocket and rebounded with bouquets of spirit and smiles that are contagious. We have overcome the difficulties which life has presented and turned them into "bouquets of golden flowers."

Just like that roadside border of flowers, there is something so indomitable and beautiful when we realize and appreciate the strength and wisdom of the ever increasing number of friends and neighbors in our own community who are living and loving the second fifty years of their life.

The solution to the challenge of *age* lies in our commitment to a personal change of attitude and expectation for happiness. Commit today to change those negative attitudes about being older that society presents you.

Take charge of your *aging* process. You can do it and you will love it! Promise yourself that your spirit will not grow gray before your hair! As a positive member of the fastest growing group of people in our population, you will be the victorious yellow bouquet of blossoms along the highway we call life.

Take care and God bless!

Patterns on the Parkway

Remember the movie "Close Encounters of the Third Kind"? While driving on Old Fort Parkway last week, something happened that could be described as a *close encounter* of the "life kind"! Now, the Parkway has been much maligned of late. The congestion, construction, and general concern for safety of self and car are but a few of the conversations that buzz around the dinner tables. This thoroughfare has become a challenging stretch of roadway.

On this particular day, around lunchtime, I was late leaving Murfreesboro for a meeting in Nashville. I found myself in the usual routine of breath holding and finger tapping, while waiting for the green arrow so I could turn left from Broad Street onto the Parkway. Getting on to the Parkway was the beginning of this *close encounter of the life kind.*

It was a familiar story of stopping and starting, switching lanes, and missing green lights. It was a day of stalled cars and emergency vehicles, speeding automobiles, and slow as molasses moving trucks. In truth, it did not take nearly as much time as it seemed to get to the I-24 access ramp and head toward Nashville. It just felt like it took forever!

It was just about this time that the second life encounter occurred. As I finally veered off to the right leaving the suffocating Parkway behind and heading out onto the Interstate, there was an overwhelming sense of relief and achievement, a feeling of unconstrained freedom to move on with my plans for the day.

What had occurred in those few moments was an emotional encounter remarkably similar to what happens in life. A trip on Old Fort Parkway can be a classic demonstration of the cycles of life. It was all the snapshots in our photo albums about who we are and what we do.

Just as we wait for the green arrow to get onto the Parkway, expectant parents wait for what seems like endless days, for the birth of that first child. We switch lanes, stop and start, go slow, and sometimes back up. In life, we move to new homes, change jobs or careers, stop for a moment to rethink our goals, go back to school or move to new communities.

This particular piece of highway has

several names... Highway 96, Memorial Boulevard, and Lebanon Road. In life, we take a married name, add a title to the name, are referred to by nicknames, and sometimes retake a former name.

Along Old Fort Parkway, there is a sampling of the most things we think are essential to our life. We can have meals together, be entertained, and buy supplies to build our homes or find shelter for the night. We can find the same things for ourselves with families and communities.

Just as there were stalled vehicles and accidents on the road that were being attended to by the appropriate officials, in life, we have accidents. We called them mistakes. Often our car may overheat under the stress of highway travel. We often overheat under life's pressure. Sometimes we lose a career or lose a friend. Then we use the professional help of physicians and counselors to get our lives back on track.

When things are really tough, we need that special person who will let us have the right of way... or who shows us an extra bit of compassion. Sympathetic drivers allow us to get in front of them or pull out from a side street even though traffic is bumper to bumper.

In life we find many people who show such good manners and neighborliness that it makes our journey through life a joy. In life, as on the Parkway, we sometimes just cannot figure out where we are supposed to go. Drivers on the Parkway often roll down their car windows to give directions and a word of encouragement when we need it the most.

The old adage... "Saving the best for last," was quite true in this *encounter* with life. We pass through all the stages of life from infancy to adulthood, coping with one hang up after another, much like we managed to get from Broad Street to I-24. The familiar access ramp is like life at retirement age.

According to statistics, we have a third of our life left to enjoy after we retire. It can be smooth sailing compared to the challenging years of rearing children or building a career. With a little bit of planning ahead of time for our traveling on the retirement parkway of our life, the light is green. Be sure to take a few minutes to get out the road maps and work out the "traffic jams" before arriving at that special stage of adulthood!

One thing is for sure. When you finally get to the interstate and experience the freedom and exhilaration of this destination, the last thing you want is to have to park your car and watch others who go on by without you!

Retirement can be just the beginning of another wonderful close encounter with life!

Patterns of Patriotism

Several hundred years ago, John Fawcett used the phrase "...tie that binds our hearts..." to compose a beautiful hymn. Today, it is as familiar to most of us as it was to our great-grandparents many years ago. Those lyrics are most often associated with worship services and Sunday mornings, but it is certain that Fawcett's song has been played or sung on a variety of occasions other than in church.

Last week, there was an opportunity to be present at the Rotary Club for a Salute to Veterans. For some reason of which I'm not really sure, this particular tribute was so moving and special for both the group of veterans being saluted and the grateful audience in attendance. Thoughts

of patriotism seemed to be accompanied
by silent melodies of sacred music and the
powerful lines of Fawcett's hymn.

There were few in attendance with dry
eyes and many grateful hearts being bound
together during the Salute. There were
feelings of admiration and respect for those
veterans who, in ways we will never be
able to understand, know what war really
is. During the recognition of those soldiers
from World War II to those who saw combat
through the Vietnam era and to those who
proudly wear a uniform today, a different
sense of the meaning "...tie that binds our
hearts..." took center stage. The "ties"
between those soldiers were so profound.
The younger and the older stood together;
there was no "generation gap" in that group.
On full array and for all of us to see was the
essence of intergenerational strength and

understanding.

One particular WWII veteran was flanked on one side by his daughter and on the other side by his grandson. After all these years, he is still a hero of the finest kind. He continues to be the living example of "an officer and a gentleman" and his adult grandson's real-life hero. The uncompromising respect for this WWII survivor is a legacy that has stood the test of time. It is a powerful "tie that binds" the generations in this family together in a very special way.

On meaningful display for each of us to see was a beautiful example of aging. These men and women did their work in times and places that even then were worlds apart. They performed their military service in different parts of the world and under extraordinarily different circumstances. Yet on this day, there was no distance between them. They seemed to have an unspoken yet unmistakable command of common purpose and mutual respect. They are survivors bound together in the history of our country.

The "ties that bind" these hearts were not only for each of those present. They were bound by thoughts of fallen soldiers whose memories can still call forth tears. The remembered pals and friends, sons and daughters, spouses and family members are also forever joined by the ties that bind us together as a community and a country. This was, indeed, an American moment.

On this November 11th, in a world that has become individualized by special interest groups, support groups, income levels, age groups, and political persuasions, our lives were all made richer by the tie that binds our hearts to those we know and miss and to those we do not know who paid the ultimate price. On this Veterans Day, it was youth and age in perfect alignment.

In the finest sense of military "family" we have great reason to be optimistic about the future when treasures from both our past and present continue to be so valued and remembered. Maggie Britton Vaughn, the Poet Laureate of Tennessee, wrote the following about our flag. *"... I've been hurled, furled, and twirled in every way that you can; I've been scorned, torn, worn, and burned across this land. But as long as there's a July 4th and a Veterans Day parade, as long as there's a ballgame, Old Glory's got it made. As long as there's a hand to place on the heart; as long as there's a bugle to play "Taps" before dark. As long as there's a country and dawns' early light, as long as there's an American..."*

To the veterans, young and old, thank you for the "ties that bind our hearts" together and allow us to feel such pride.

Flight
Patterns

There are spectacular moments in nature that compel us to simply stop what we are doing and take notice. Sighting a flock of geese flying in that familiar "V" formation for example, is something grand to see. If you happen to spot them in the night sky against one of those crystal bright winter moons, it almost takes your breath! Even among seasoned hunters, few will deny that to quietly observe the flight of geese as they move in and out of the wildlife areas right at daybreak or to watch them as the late afternoon sun sits huge on the horizon, is one of the highlights of a hunting adventure.

Several days ago, I spotted some of these magnificent waterfowl. This flock of geese was flying with an almost total control of

the elements in seemingly effortless style. I
couldn't get that sight out of my mind! Here
I was in a traffic jam, rendered immobile.
There they were moving ahead on their
course with determination and control.
Here I was, with many others, revving our
engines, but we were going nowhere fast.
There they were with the *"wind beneath their
wings"* moving elegantly and silently on a
highway with no orange and white barrels
or traffic lights or construction equipment!
How can this be?

Looking up at them you could not help but
sense the strength of the span of their wings
and that committed instinct to achieve
the ultimate destination of the journey.
Their struggle with distance, with fatigue,
and with the unknown did not deter them
one little bit. What's more, they appeared
entirely unaffected by the fact that many

of us were sitting in our cars, with engines running hot, watching them in awe. It is curious how you can have such a positive feeling about so tiny a neighbor in this amazing world of nature.

Geese have some other characteristics of flight that are lesser known than their formation. The leader in this flight pattern stays in the key position until it becomes too weary to continue. Then, without much ado, it simply relinquishes the lead spot and drops back into the formation with the group. A new leader who is more rested and has the renewed perseverance to assume responsibility for the group and the flight pattern makes its way to the front. This is a role of continuous leadership and teamwork about which most organizations and groups could only dream.

How these beautiful creatures
instinctively maintain that perfect balance
with each other and as a group must
be nature at its best. Hours later, as the
memories of that pattern of geese just
drifted around in my mind, there was a
feeling that I was overlooking something.
Finally, what I had not been able to see
became clear. Geese were not the only
species in nature that had a special pattern
for travel. In the grand design of nature,
there had not been a failure to instill the
human family with an equally beautiful
gift of formation for travel through life.
It happens everyday! We see it everyday!
Maybe we are simply too busy sitting in our
personal and collective traffic jams to notice.

In our own families and communities, we
see those folks who are forty, fifty, sixty, and
even seventy as they act in the lead position

for all kinds of activities. They have the experience, the education, the dreams, the physical stamina and the determination to chart the course for the rest of us.

While they lead, just as with the geese, there are those standing shoulder to shoulder with them, *"waiting in the wings,"* (no pun intended) ready to step up to the task should they receive the call. Similarly, our leaders are flanked on one side by those who are more senior in age and on the other side by those who are younger. Both are essential to the necessary balance to stay the course.

At all the appropriate and necessary places along this journey of daily living, the person in the lead position will drop back into the group for rest and renewal. No matter which age group receives the call to assume the pivotal front position, the lead will belong to the one that has a zest for life. It will go to one with a spirit for adventure that is strong and unaffected by those who choose to sit and watch. It will fall on one who is committed to making each new morning the beginning of a great new day.

The lead will go to those who with the strength of character to take the hand of someone who is physically weary from the journey or emotionally weakened by the struggle against the wind. The leader will, almost instinctively, pull them along on the trip until they can again fly by themselves. It is, as if on cue, the right person who always answers the call to go to the front of the "V" and continue the flight. Sometimes it is the younger one with the dreams of making a difference. Sometimes, it may be the older one whose wisdom, understanding, and experience will make the difference in the success or failure to achieve our goals.

It may be important to remember that those incredibly beautiful geese we chance to see are probably exhausted as they continue to fly on their course. From our position, we only see that gentle, graceful motion of their body and hear a silent brush of their wings against the wind. It is so easy to appreciate those things we do not see too often, but we should be careful not to take the special, though familiar gifts of everyday living for granted.

For just a moment, though we are weary and have thoughts of giving up, we may reflect on those familiar patterns of support and encouragement from friends and family and folks we may not even know. May we keep in our memory a simple perspective on the geometry of aging learned one day from a mere flock of geese!

The thought is this: It takes both lines in the "V" formation for it to work properly for the geese. In the effective process of aging, it takes both the young and old in our families and in our communities if we are to be successful on our journey through life in this wonderful place we call home.

Trees in Winter

M ost of our houses have that special window that just invites us to sit down and take a peak outside. We can watch the world go by, the seasons come and go, and the neighborhood children literally grow up before our very eyes.

We have a place like that in our old house. It is one of those quaint Victorian-type windows that juts out from the rest of the house. Whether you are just walking by and take a look outside or choose to sit down for a while, you experience a different kind of connection with the world. You are at eye level with the birds flying in and out of the trees. You are looking through the trees rather than up at them.

The view from this window is something that reminds you of the Swiss Family Robinson's tree house. We have been watching the world from our upstairs window for almost twenty-seven years. Maybe it's because the view is more interesting through lace curtains, but then again, it may just be the view itself.

You could almost say that, because of these special windows and others like them in our house, each of us can have season tickets to a performance of nature that is unmatched in New York or Hollywood. The sights and sounds become more and more meaningful as the pages of our lives are played out. There is so much power in nature, and trees are at the heart of it all. One writer put it like this ... "If you would know strength and patience, welcome the company of trees."

For all the years we've been admiring the trees on our property, one tree, in particular, out by the road, seems to have sustained a special attraction. Every spring it puts on a display of blossoms which perfume the morning, and every summer it gives us leaf cover to provide shade from the heat. All of this is followed by a show of brilliant color in the fall. But what was it about this tree in winter? There is a message there; one I was not connected with until now.

Looking out our window, there it stood. Without a single leaf, it looked rather stark against a blue November sky. You could see where some limbs had been damaged by winters or storms. Several were even broken off. This tree wasn't quite as tall as it had been. Certainly, it was not as tall as some of the other younger trees. In much the same way we say about ourselves, this tree was showing its age.

Trees are not just the blossoms of spring, nor the leaves of fall, we anticipate and enjoy. A tree is that bark-covered trunk and all its infinite system of limbs and branches that reaches toward the sun. A tree is the vast root system that provides its strength and support and holds the soil around it in place. The leaves and blossoms and all the "jillion" other things that we love about trees are just extras in the performance of nature at play.

The message of the "tree in winter" has significance to us because we are inextricably a part of nature. Trees are a reflection of us. Throughout our life, we are also building limbs and branches of character that reach upward. We build systems of roots in family tradition and strong values which hold our lives in place.

Even with some broken limbs, trees are still an active participant in nature's choreography of life that goes on day after day and season after season. As we age, we may have a broken limb or a health disorder, but we continue to remain engaged in daily living with joy and confidence.

We can take another lesson from that "tree in winter." Many times our real strength can be hidden behind seasonal costumes of leaves and blossoms. Like the tree, it is what we are beneath the clothes and makeup that is the important part of who we are and what we are about.

Season after season and year after year, we are a player in the performance of life. If you happen to have a broken limb or such, just put on a wool sweater, stay warm, and keep going. Spring will come.

Patterns in Time

While trying to write some thoughts on resolutions for the New Year, it just simply wouldn't happen! What would happen is the new clock we received for Christmas would chime a beautiful little melody. Any ideas being developed quickly turned to this simple little reminder of the *time*. Listening to that clock chime on the hour had almost the same emotional effect one feels when you hear church bells tolling in the distance.

Many of us, myself included, did not grow up with, nor have as a part of our home even in our adult life, a grandfather clock or other chiming time piece. Having this clock has been an extraordinary experience. This reproduction of an antique school clock has become the Christmas gift that may last a *"lifetime."* No pun intended!

The clock and its chime sequence offer several points to ponder about this phenomenon of nature. There must be hundreds of literary references about time and its value as well as its passing. The hour glass with the sand flowing into the bottom container is a familiar reference point for works of art. One of the lines from a piece of music by Jim Croce goes something like, "... if I could put time in a bottle..." If only!

The dictionary defines "time" as a continuous measurable quantity in which events occur in apparently irreversible order. In the course of daily living, some of us seem to have too much time on our hands. Others of us never seem to have enough. Some of us assume we have years and years left in our life span. Others, because of health situations, understand and accept that the number of their days has been quantified.

Einstein described an appreciation of the tiniest portion of this measurement. I hope he will pardon my unscientific liberty with his theories! He observed that even one minute of time with your hand too close to the flame of a candle is an unbelievably long amount of time. On the other hand, that same single minute spent with a loved one is hardly enough to catch your breath.

In discussing time, someone wrote that all of our memories create our past. Our imagination is our future. In between these two is a tiny slither of time we call today! No matter how much time to live we believe we have, all we really know is about today. One twenty-four hour period during which clocks and time pieces will continue to chime is a fantastic opportunity, whether we are eighteen or eighty, to achieve something wonderful. It may be the smallest notion or the grandest success, but it is ours to do with as we choose.

There is a side bar to this story about time. The new clock chimes on the fifteen minute intervals. These sounds are a gentle, beautiful way to remind one that time is silently, unrelentingly passing so quickly! It is also a private reminder that we are a part of a universe grander and more incredible than our imagination can grasp. This gift of time we have been given is our connection to this magnificent creation.

Perhaps, we should resolve this year to carry "a bottle of time" in our memory bank as a daily reminder of how precious this gift really is. So instead of those traditional resolutions for the New Year, an energized appreciation for our gift of time may help achieve some special little miracles during these three hundred sixty plus days of life we hope to live during the upcoming year. Make today, and all your tomorrows, great ones!

Time for a Christmas Gift

The pieces of work concerning Christmas can hardly be counted. Renditions of written and creative thinking about Christmas, the holidays and Santa have been around for centuries and the volumes continue to increase. Bookstores and libraries are bulging with seasonal favorites by authors ranging from children to the masters. An amateur writer could be intimidated by the magical, whimsical nature of this vast collection. To presume that there might be something new to create that would measure up and be of interest is a little bold.

That being said ... plug in your tree lights and turn on some Christmas music. Santa has something to say to those folks who

can identify with his white hair and similar
physique. Perhaps he has been waiting
for us to grow old enough to appreciate a
Christmas message that can only be heard
during this special stage in life.

The spirit of Santa is about gifts and
giving. The magic of Santa is about laughter
and smiles. It is about hugs for children and
caring for even the tiniest creatures among
us. It is about a youthful anticipation of pure
joy on Christmas morning. I came across a
line written by P. B. Shelley, "Hope will make
thee young for hope and youth are children
of one mother." Wow!

If Shelly is right, we have only to reclaim
that hope we had on Christmas Eve to regain
the energy of our youth, something the spirit
of Santa can help us with. He really does
have a thing or two to teach those of us who

are in the second half of this *holiday on
earth we call life.* We have been leaving the
lessons of Santa for the children to learn for
all these years, yet all the while he has been
ringing his silent bells of Christmas hoping
that the "grown-ups" and the "grown-olders"
were listening.

The spirit of Santa is a legacy for our
family, friends and all those whose lives
we touch on our trip through life. It is a
personality and a philosophy of living that
is filled with gifts of joy and laughter.
Humor is the prescription of choice for
faces that find it so difficult to really smile.
Joy is the message of Santa's silent bells
that fills us with hope and anticipation for
Christmas morning.

C. W. Rodgers is one of those people who
had that spirit. When his hair was white, he

wrote a book titled, <u>Twentieth Century USA – A Ludicrous History</u>, that defines his gift of laughter and sense of joy. It is a legacy for his family. The following introduction to his book is C. W. at his best:

This history, written in my ninetieth year, is from my memory with a little help on statistics and dates from the World Book Encyclopedia. It is written in response to questions from those too young to be aware of many of the events that have shaped our country during this century. So, for those under eighty, I give an easy to read account colored by my own philosophy. Those over eighty probably do not need to read this, but I hope you will anyway. Bless you, and I hope your history is as ludicrous and as much fun as my own.

This is the kind of zest for life and adventure that allows us to enjoy being older.

He understood that hope and a youthful spirit are a gift you first give to yourself and then go on to share with others. C. W. really heard Santa's silent Christmas bells of cheer. He left them for his family and others of us to hear in his writings. May we all hear those silent Christmas bells that only ring for us grown-ups! Merry Christmas!

The Between Times

During the holidays, it seemed like green wreaths and red bows were everywhere ... funny, how the combination of these two colors has such special significance in our lives. On the one hand, Christmas greenery and red ribbons of all sizes welcome in holidays and celebrations that can warm even the coldest winter night. On the other hand, red and green is a modern symbol of traffic control and social rules and regulations. The lyrics of one favorite Christmas song describes these street lights as a part of Christmas, "dressed in bright red and green."

The older we get, the more we can find connections in everything. If there is just a bit more room left in your heart to reflect on the holiday season, consider this. Almost as soon as the last gift is opened on Christmas, we emotionally begin the process of packing up the decorations and making some resolutions for the New Year. Newspapers and magazines, not only in our town, but around the world, are filled with articles on why and how to successfully ring in the New Year.

What about those seven days between Christmas and New Year's Day? Putting together a Christmas, from the smallest celebration to the grandest, involves a huge amount of planning and work. We tend to begin the tasks earlier each year with hopes of having more time to enjoy our labor of love. A friend suggested that maybe December is not big enough to hold Christmas! Maybe so, but the "week between" offers some real opportunity.

We could find a message in the red and green colors of Christmas. The greenery represents all the hustle, bustle, preparation, gift buying, house cleaning, cooking and entertaining. The red bows are a beautiful way of saying to ourselves and those we love to just "stop." Stop and take advantage of the "week between." We have one hundred and sixty-eight hours to relive the glory of the Christmas season and to really experience the joy of the holidays.

We can use the red bow to gently remind us that the "week between" is also significant in our extraordinary journey through the aging process. There are lots of "between times" in life that can be overflowing with opportunities and achievements. If we are "tuned in" long enough, we can find special little miracle times that are tucked in among big events.

The times between the visits of children and grandchildren, of family get-togethers and the times between the loss of friends and loved ones all hold unusual moments for personal growth and a renewed spirit. It is these "between times" when we relearn the importance of sharing and giving, of focus and self-reliance.

According to some, over one-third of our lives are lived after retirement. That is a pretty big "time between." Who we are and what we do reflects our respect for life itself. We have heard that a mind is a terrible thing to waste. Even more tragic is to waste even one wonderful day of living in this time we call our "old age!" Growing older requires the strongest spunk. It requires the most well-trained attitude. It requires a resilience that can be fine tuned during those "times between."

Taking note of our between times allows us to peek in on our tomorrows while making the absolute most of the priceless gift of our todays. As you begin to box up your holiday treasures, enjoy a few minutes to find a connection in the week between two wonderful celebrations. It just might become the best week of the year and all those that await us in the future.

About the Author

Becci Bookner founded her first successful service company addressing the needs of seniors in 1993 and is the Founder and President of Family Staffing Solutions, Inc. She previously created and developed an Extended School Program (ESP) childcare pilot project which provided before and after school child care utilizing school property. The project now serves as a national model and has been the subject of major media attention as reported on Good Morning America and U.S. News and World Report.

She has received the Quality of Life Award presented by the U.S. House of Representatives Small Business Committee.

Patterns of the Heart: Gentle Thoughts on Aging is Ms. Bookner's first book, followed by *Good Manners for Great Caregivers: Gaining an Exceptional Edge.* She has several other books scheduled for publication this year.

Ms. Bookner is a nationally renowned speaker and consultant on care giving issues and is available for speaking engagements and national interviews.